ALICE
in
WONDERLAND

D1629514

Bath New York Singapore Hong Kong Cologne Delhi Melbourne

The Unbirthday Song
Music and Lyrics by Mack David, Al Hoffman and Jerry Livingston
© 1948 Walt Disney Music Company (ASCAP). © renewed. All rights reserved.
International © secured.

I'm Late
Music by Sammy Fain
Lyrics by Bob Hilliard
© 1949 Walt Disney Music Company (ASCAP). © renewed. All rights reserved.
International © secured.
℗ 2005 Walt Disney Records

This edition published by Parragon in 2010

Parragon
Queen Street House
4 Queen Street
Bath BA1 1HE, UK

ISBN 978-1-4454-4156-6

Printed in China

This is the story of Alice in
Wonderland.
You can read along with me in your
book. You will know it is time to turn
the page when you hear this sound...

Let's begin now:

Do you know where Wonderland is? It's the place you visit in your dreams – that strange and wondrous land where nothing is as it seems. Alice learned all about Wonderland one warm, golden afternoon when she fell asleep under a cool, shady tree.

The first strange thing that Alice saw in
Wonderland was a white rabbit wearing pants and
a waistcoat! He rushed down the path, glancing
hurriedly at his watch.

"I'm late. I'm late for a very important date. No
time to say hello, goodbye. I'm late, I'm late, I'm late,
I'm late!"

Alice watched him scurry across a brook and disappear into a hollow tree.

"Now, this is curious. What could a rabbit possibly be late for? It must be a party or something."

Alice crossed the brook and peered into the hollow tree.

"What a peculiar place to have a party!"

She squeezed through the opening and found herself crawling down a dark tunnel.

"I really shouldn't do this. After all, I haven't been invited. And curiosity often leads to trouble..." The tunnel floor abruptly ended, and Alice fell down a large hole!

But it wasn't a dirty, musty hole. It was like a tall, thin house. There were bookshelves and cupboards and pictures on the wall. And Alice was falling very slowly, so she had time to look around and think.

"Hmm. What if I should fall right through the centre of the earth and come out the other side?"

Alice landed with a bump, just in time to see the White Rabbit disappear through a tiny door.

"Oh, Mister Rabbit. Wait, please!"

Alice squeezed through the door and found herself outside again.

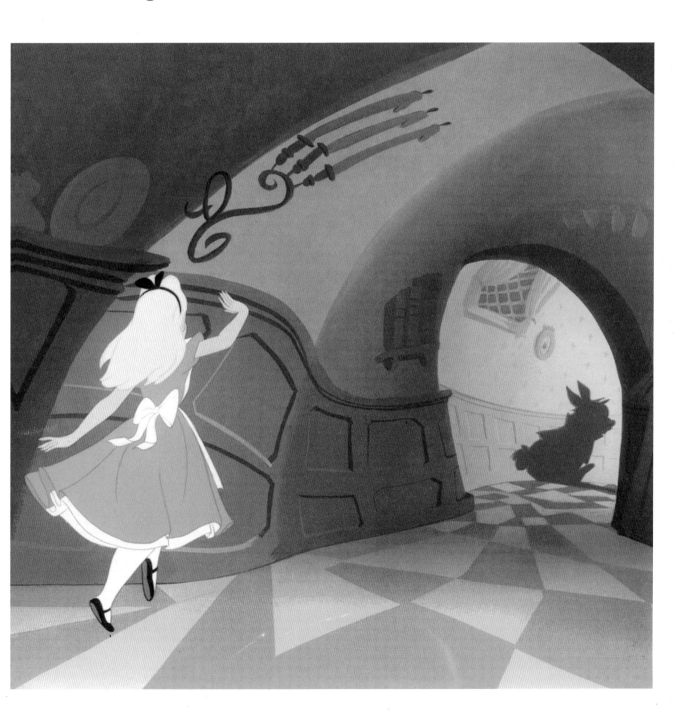

"Oh, dear, I'm sure the White Rabbit came this way."
But when Alice looked around, she found everything
either upside-down or backwards.

"Curiouser and curiouser," thought Alice.

Stranger still, whenever Alice would eat a bit of cake or take a sip to drink, she would change sizes! Once, a bite of mushroom sent her shooting up in height. Her head cleared the treetops and frightened the birds nesting there.

Another bite made Alice shrink so small that the
flowers and the rocking-horse-fly towered above her.

Alice also met talking animals in Wonderland. There was the Walrus and the Dodo and the Caterpillar. They tried to help Alice with her search for the White Rabbit.

But they mainly took up her time with funny songs and silly races. "Forward, backward, inward, outward, bottom to the top! Makes no difference where you run as long as you don't stop!"

So Alice went off to find the White Rabbit by herself.

Alice came to a clearing, and there stood a
small house with pink shutters and a round door.
"Now I wonder who lives here?" thought Alice.

Just then, the front door flew open, and out raced the White Rabbit!

"Oh me, oh my. I'm awfully late! My fuzzy ears and whiskers took me too much time to shave!"

The White Rabbit looked up to see Alice at the garden gate.

"Why, Mary Ann! What are you doing here? Well don't just do something, stand there! No, no, no – go get my gloves! I'm late!"

"But late for what?" asked Alice.

"My gloves!" said the White Rabbit firmly. So Alice dutifully went to look for them, though she knew full well that she wasn't Mary Ann!

When Alice came back, the White Rabbit was just disappearing through the woods again.

"You see, I'm overdue – I'm in a rabbit stew! Can't even say goodbye, hello. I'm late, I'm late, I'm late!"

Alice rushed off into the woods again, only this time, she was greeted by a funny pair of twins named Tweedledum and Tweedledee.

"Say, 'How do you do' and shake hands. State your name and business!"

When Alice said her business was finding the White Rabbit, the two sillies directed her to the Mad Hatter's tea party.

"Sit down and join us, my dear," said the Mad Hatter.

"Since it's not our birthdays today, the March Hare and I decided to celebrate our unbirthdays!"

"Why, then it's my unbirthday today, too!" exclaimed Alice. And they all celebrated with tea and cake.

Alice left the party and next came to a lovely garden where playing cards were working as gardeners. They were all busy painting the roses red. "Why must you do that?" Alice asked the three-of-clubs.

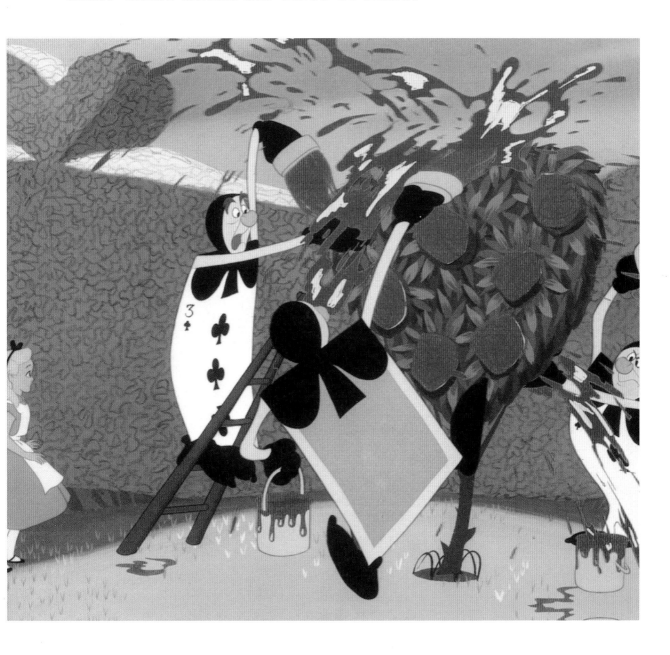

"We planted white roses by mistake, and the Queen will have our heads unless we change them all to red!"

A trumpet blew, and the cards all scampered into line.

"Make way for the Queen of Hearts!" Called a familiar voice.

Alice peeked around a card to see the White Rabbit leading the royal procession.

"So this is why he was hurrying so!"

Then Alice spotted the ill-tempered Queen and her timid little husband. Behind them followed a file of stern-looking playing cards.

"Who is this?" Snapped the Queen, pointing to Alice.

"Why, it's a little girl. Do you play croquet?" Alice curtsied.

"Yes, Your Majesty. But I really mustn't stay. I'm trying to find my way home."

"Your way?" Bellowed the Queen.

"All ways here are my ways. Off with her head!"

The Queen's cards rushed at Alice to carry out their orders!

"Oh, pooh. I'm not afraid of you! Why, you're nothing but a pack of cards."

Alice gave the cards a push, and they went flying in all directions.

This made the Queen very angry.

"Off with her head!" She roared, and the cards regrouped for another charge!

Suddenly, Alice woke up and found herself still under the shady tree.

"Why, it was all a dream. Thank goodness. I've had quite enough of Wonderland for now."